Anne Underhill

A Most Peculiar Day

Illustrated by Dusica Dimitrovska

Anne Underhill

A Most Peculiar Day

Illustrated by

Dusica Dimitrovska

Design and Layout

Koma.lab

www.koma.com.mk

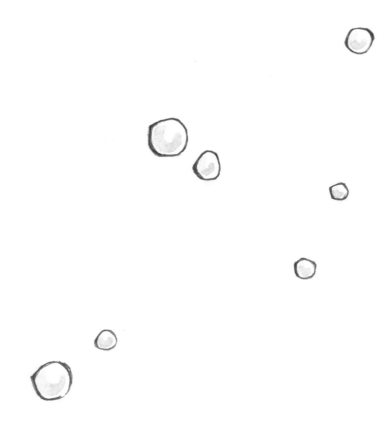

For Edith and Edward with all my love

Mummy

The hottest day, the sun is out,
I'm in my pool splashing about.
Above the fence, what should appear?
A great grey trunk and 2 big ears!

The Elephant says, "I don't suppose,
You'd let me stick my big long nose,
Into your pool?" Then with a sigh,
The watering hole has gone all dry."

"Of course!" I say "You tuck right in!"
And then in looms a chomping chin,
A great long neck, a nervous laugh.
"Erm...hello there," says the Giraffe.

"Not to be rude, but do you think,
That I could also have a drink?"

Who's coming next? I'd like to know.
Up pops a hairy Buffalo.

Someone swings down from the tree,
"Good afternoon!" Says Chimpanzee.

A Rhino charges through the gate,
He shouts, "I hope I'm not too late!"

8

Hippo groans, "It hurts to swallow,
I'm too hot and need to wallow!"

Blurry stripes go whizzing by,
Then Zebra whinnies, "My throats dry!"

A Lion roars, "I've got a thirst!
I'm the King! I should go first!"

Some Meerkats scamper from the flowers.
"We've been waiting here for hours!"

They start to push and shove and slurp.
They shout and splash and belch and burp.

"STOP IT!" I shout, "Stop right away!
Just listen to me, look this way!
None of you has any manners!
This might do in the Savannah,
but it's no way to behave!"

I carry on I'm feeling brave.

16

"Now make a line and
wait your turn. You
animals all need to learn.
It's not okay to push in
front. To spit and slurp
and burp and grunt!

18

You all know what you have to do,
get into line and form a queue."

I'm dinner now, I think, but wait!

No, being munched is not my fate!

A moment later, shuffling feet. They form a line that's nice and neat. Some have a splash, some take a dip. Some drink a gulp and some a sip.

23

And when they're done, they all go home,
My pool is dry, I'm all alone.
"It's dinner time," I hear mum say.

What a most peculiar day!

Did you know?

Elephant

An elephant's trunk is its most important limb. It's so sensitive it can pick up a blade of grass, but it's so strong it can rip the branches from a tree. Elephants are great swimmers and use their trunks like a snorkel.
Can you pretend to be an elephant with a long trunk?

Giraffe

Although it's very long, a giraffe's neck only has seven bones or vertebrae, the same as us.
Just like some small children I know, giraffes only need between five and 30 minutes sleep a day.

Buffalo

Buffaloes weigh up to 2000 pounds (almost the weight of a small car). Despite their huge size they mainly eat grass. They need to eat a lot of it, so they're on the move for around 18 hours a day and with herds of hundreds sometimes more, that's a lot of grass!
Pretend to be a buffalo munching the grass!

Chimpanzee

Chimpanzees or "chimps" are human's closest relatives. They're very clever and can use tools like sticks and rocks to dig out bugs and smash nutshells. In 1961, before any people had been to space, they sent a chimp named Ham to find out how our bodies might react.

Rhinoceros

Rhinos have really bad eyesight, so even though they're gigantic and have big frightening horns, they are easily scared and charge at whatever gets them spooked, even if it's just a rock or a tree.

Can you charge like a rhino?

Their horns are made of keratin, the same stuff as our finger and toenails.

Hippopotamus

Hippos can't swim! They move through the water by walking or bouncing along the river bed or pushing off from other objects and gliding.

Hippos can close their nostrils and ears to stop water getting in and they can hold their breath for up to 7 minutes.

How long can you hold your breath?

Zebra

Zebras coats often look like they are white with black stripes, but underneath the fur, the skin is black.

There are lots of reasons we think zebras may have their stripes. It could be for camouflage, to keep away bloodsucking bugs, to deter predators and a whole host of other theories but nobody really knows for sure.

Lion

Lions can sleep for up to 20 hours a day but when they are awake it's the female lions who do almost all of the hunting. Once they've done all the hard work, it's the males who get to eat first!

A lion's roar is so loud it can be heard up to 5 miles away.

How loud can you roar?

Meerkat

Meerkats live in burrows up to 5 meters deep, with lots of tunnels and openings.

They take it in turns to be the "sentry" and be on lookout to check for predators while the others forage for food.

Can you pretend to be a meerkat on lookout?

Printed in Great Britain
by Amazon